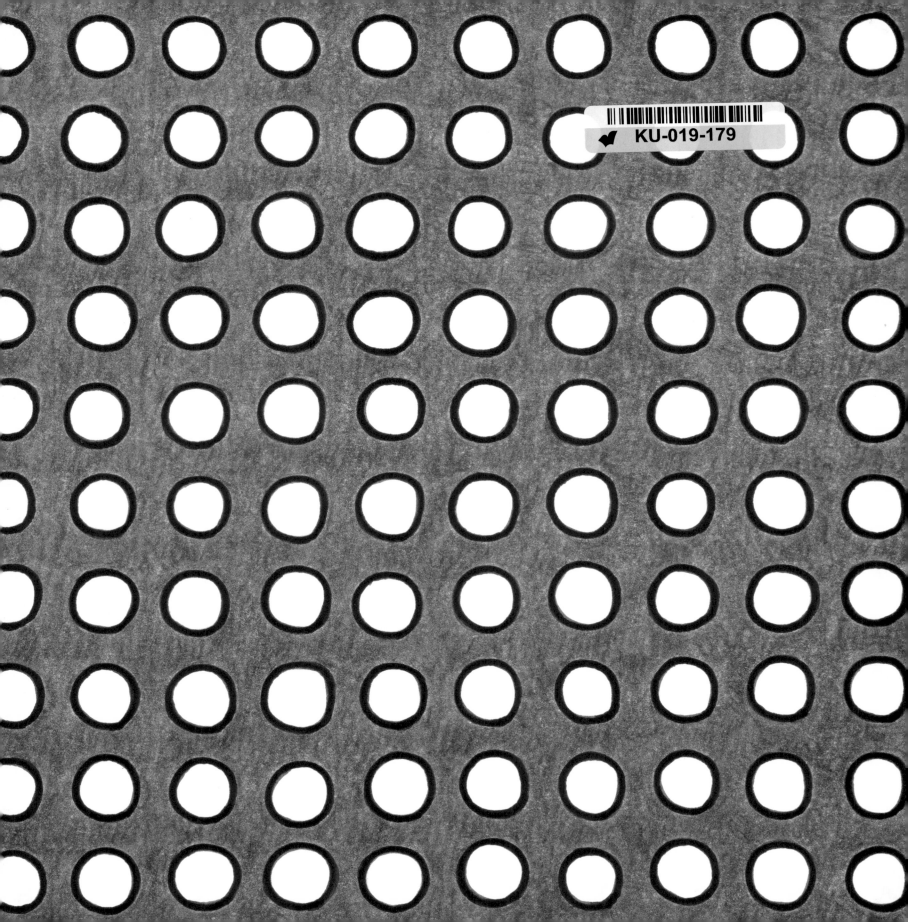
KU-019-179

Kitten's First Full Moon

KEVIN HENKES
Kitten's
First

Full Moon

SIMON AND SCHUSTER

London   New York   Sydney

For L, W, C & S

First published in Great Britain in 2006 by Simon & Schuster UK Ltd
Africa House, 64-78 Kingsway, London WC2B 6AH
A CBS COMPANY
Originally published in 2004 by Greenwillow Books, an imprint of HarperCollins Publishers
Copyright © 2004 Kevin Henkes
The text for this book is set in Gill Sans
The illustrations for this book are rendered in gouache and coloured pencil
A CIP catalogue record for this book is available from the British Library upon request

ISBN 1 416 91108 1
EAN 9781416911081

Printed in China

10 9 8 7 6 5 4 3 2 1

It was Kitten's first full moon.

When she saw it, she thought,

There's a little bowl of milk in the sky.

And she wanted it.

So she closed her eyes
and stretched her neck
and opened her mouth and licked.

**But Kitten only ended up
with a bug on her tongue.
Poor Kitten!**

Still, there was the little bowl

of milk, just waiting.

So she pulled herself together

and wiggled her bottom

and sprang from the top step of the porch.

But Kitten only tumbled –
bumping her nose and banging her ear
and pinching her tail.
Poor Kitten!

Still, there was the little bowl

of milk, just waiting.

So she chased it –
down the sidewalk,
through the garden,
past the field,
and by the pond.
But Kitten never seemed to get closer.
Poor Kitten!

Still, there was the little bowl

of milk, just waiting.

So she ran
to the tallest tree
she could find,
and she climbed
and climbed
and climbed
to the very top.

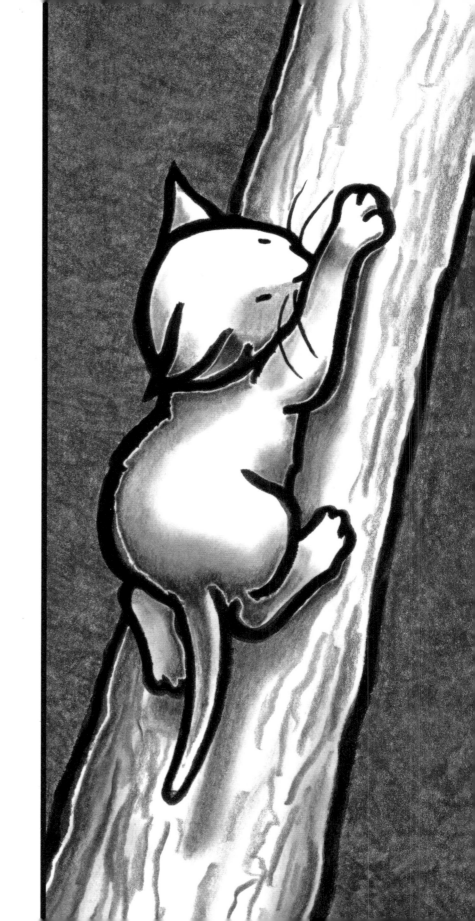

But Kitten
still couldn't reach
the bowl of milk,
and now she was
scared.
Poor Kitten!
What could she do?

Then, in the pond, Kitten saw
another bowl of milk.
And it was bigger.
What a night!

So she raced down the tree

and raced through the grass

and raced to the edge of the pond.

She leaped with all her might –

Poor Kitten!

She was wet and sad and tired and hungry.

So she went

back home –

and there was

a great big

bowl of milk

      on the porch,

just waiting for her.

Lucky Kitten!